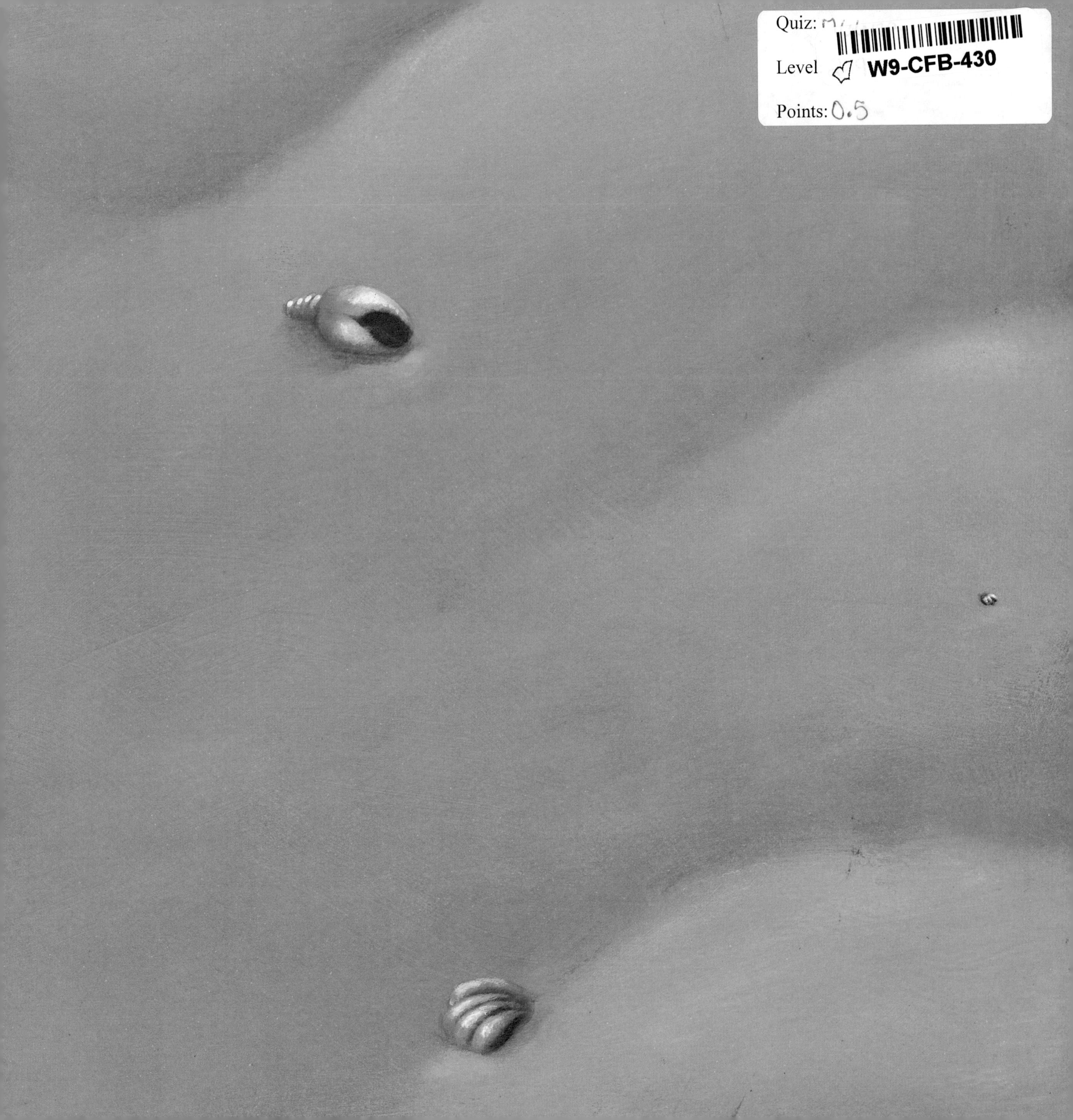

Sand Sister

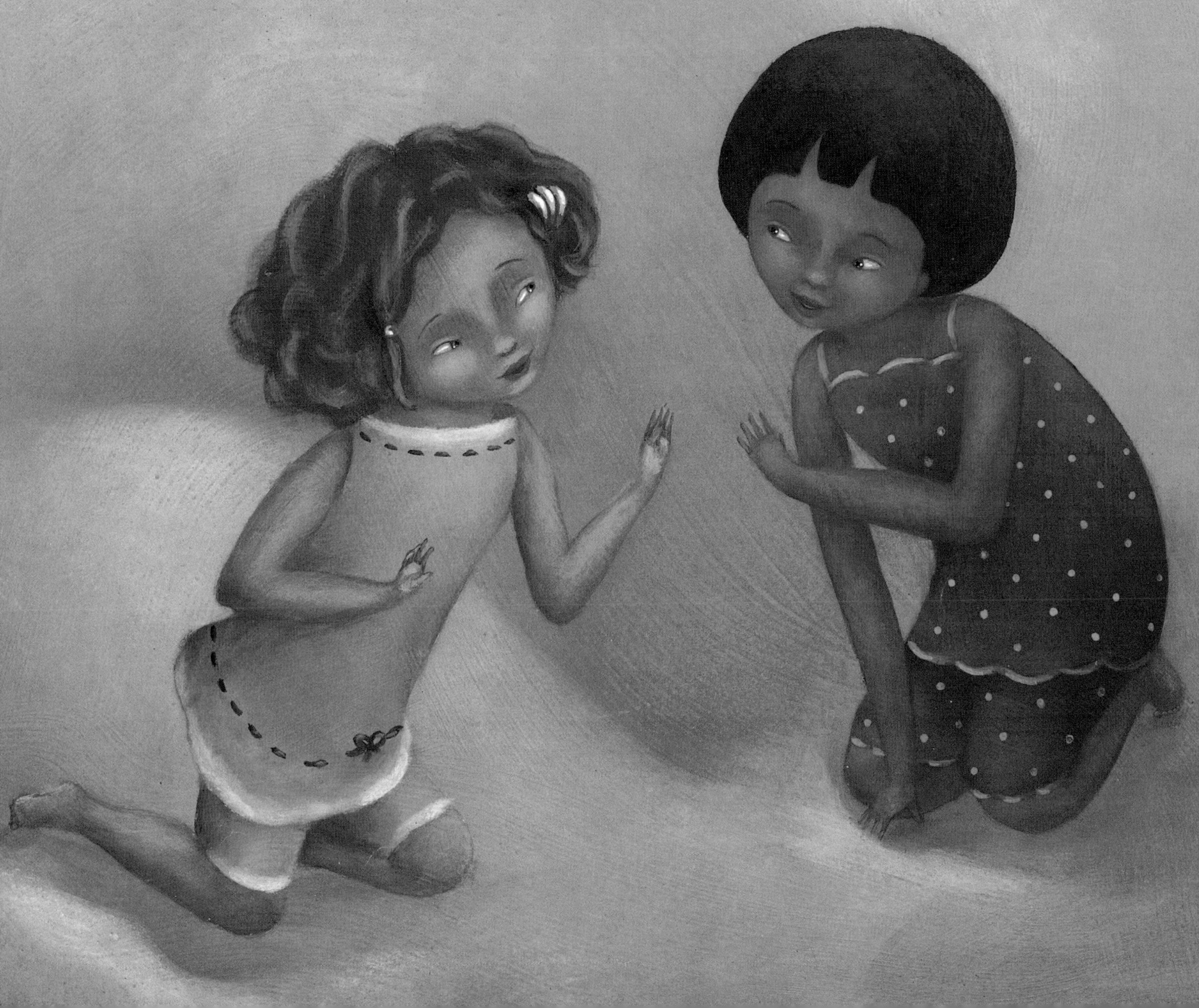

For Eva and YoYo — A.W.

For Elizabeth, Magaly, and Mario Alejandro,
my sisters of sand and my ocean brother — Y.M.

Barefoot Books, Inc.
2067 Massachusetts Ave
Cambridge, MA 02140

Text copyright © 2004 by Amanda White
Illustrations copyright © 2004 by Yuyi Morales
The moral right of Amanda White to be identified as the author
and Yuyi Morales to be identified as the illustrator of this work has been asserted

This book was typeset in Goudy Old Style 18pt on 26pt leading
The illustrations were prepared in acrylic on BFK Rives Paper

Graphic design by Barefoot Books, England
Color separation by Grafiscan, Italy
Printed and bound in China by South China Printing Ltd

This book has been printed on 100% acid-free paper

ISBN 1-84148-617-5

The Library of Congress CIP data is available under LCCN: 2003019090

1 3 5 7 9 8 6 4 2

Sand Sister

written by **Amanda White**

illustrated by **Yuyi Morales**

Barefoot Books
Celebrating Art and Story

One hot, bright summer day Paloma's Mom and Dad
told her, "We are going to a very special beach."
Sure enough, when they got there Paloma thought it
was the most beautiful place in the whole wide world.

But there was just something missing. Everyone else on the beach had brothers or sisters to play with. Paloma didn't. So instead, she found an old piece of driftwood and started drawing in the sand, all by herself. She drew another little girl, like her but with curly hair. "I wish I had a sister," she said.

"Do you really?" asked a deep voice.

"Who said that!?" Paloma spun around. All she could see was a big, old rock — and it was laughing at her!

"Meet Old Daddy Rock," it chuckled. "So you want a sister?" And the rock began to blow, softly at first and then harder, until…

…the little girl Paloma had drawn in the sand began to lift up and come to life.

Paloma was amazed and excited and amazed all over again.

"You can have your sister until the tide comes back in," said Old Daddy Rock. "And you will be the only one who can see her."

Paloma looked at Old Daddy Rock and where his
mouth had been there was just a line of limpet shells
and where his eyes had been there were two fossils.

Then she turned around to see her new sister smiling
at her. "I'm Sandra," she said to Paloma. "But you can
call me Sandy."

And oh my, there have never been two little sisters who had so much fun.

They built a boat of sand and played pirates.

They buried each other right up to their necks.

They ran after seagulls and they chased each other's shadows.

They went hunting for treasure in the rock pools and found a crab's shell.

Then they sat quietly and watched the waves and the sun on the water and held hands without thinking.

Later on, when the two girls decided to play jump-the-waves, they became silly and started pushing each other. Sandy pushed just a little too much, and Paloma fell over and was soaked right through.

"Why did you do that?" Paloma screamed. And she stormed away up the beach before Sandy could say anything.

The sisters went their separate ways. Paloma sulked and kicked at the sand. "I'm better off on my own!" she muttered.

Then she noticed that the tide was coming back in.
Soon Sandy would disappear. "Sandy! Where are you?
I'm sorry!" she shouted.

After a few moments, Sandy jumped out from behind a rock. "I missed you too," she said, with a smile on her face. Then the two girls gave each other a big, big hug.

"I have to go now," said Sandy. "I will never forget you, Paloma. Here! I found this stone with a hole in it…"

…but already Sandy was disappearing and soon all that was left of her were the feet Paloma had drawn in the sand. Before long, a big wave came and they disappeared too. The sun dipped low in the sky. Paloma shivered. She sat down by the water's edge and looked out into all that space and sky. She felt very, very small.

Soon Paloma's Mom appeared with a cardigan. "Time to go," she said.

"Shall we tell her?" asked Paloma's Dad as they started walking up the beach. Her Mom looked unsure.

"Tell me what?" asked Paloma, wishing that Sandy was still with her.

"Well," began her Mom. "You are going to have a baby brother or sister."

Paloma looked up at her parents and suddenly, she burst into tears.

"Oh Paloma!" said her Dad. "It doesn't mean we don't love you."

"I know that, Dad," Paloma sobbed. "I'm crying because I'm really, really happy."

And as she rode back to the car on her Dad's shoulders,
she curled her fingers around the stone in her pocket,
and smiled.

Barefoot Books
Celebrating Art and Story

At Barefoot Books, we celebrate art and story with books that open
the hearts and minds of children from all walks of life, inspiring them
to read deeper, search further, and explore their own creative gifts.
Taking our inspiration from many different cultures, we focus on
themes that encourage independence of spirit, enthusiasm for learning,
and acceptance of other traditions. Thoughtfully prepared by writers,
artists and storytellers from all over the world, our products combine
the best of the present with the best of the past to educate our
children as the caretakers of tomorrow.

www.barefootbooks.com